Brilliant ... Persistent

Written by Kenneth T Jolivet

ISBN: 9798 700 112 239

Edited by Melissa Peitsch

Illustrated by Renata Christine

Book Layout by Solaja Slobodan

Brilliant Bob was on
his way to school.

He walked from his house toward the big oak tree where he and his friends would meet each morning and all walk to school together.

Bob could see that Genuine George and Superboy Sam were already there.

"What's up, Brilliant Bob?" they both shouted in unison.

"Hey guys," said Bob. "Where's Dazzling Dave?"

As it turned out, Dazzling Dave was frantically running down the street, waving to his friends as he ran.

"Let's go Dave, we
don't want to be late,"
said Brilliant Bob.

Off they went, chatting about the usual things: what they watched, what they did and what they ate the night before.

Bob was describing his barbecue feast, when a boy rode past on his bike: on ONE wheel!

Brilliant Bob, Dazzling Dave, Genuine George, and Superboy Sam stopped and looked in amazement as this boy rode the "wheelie" down the block.

THE WHOLE BLOCK!

"I'm going to learn to do that," said Brilliant Bob.

"Me, too," said Dazzling Dave.

"Let's start today after school. We can practice an hour a day on our street," said Bob.

"Awesome! I can't wait," said Dazzling Dave, as they fist-bumped.

Superboy Sam and Genuine George would have to learn this skill on a bike another time.

Sam had already promised his dad he'd help paint their fence. It was a big job, which is why George had also offered to help.

A few hours later, the four friends were in math class. The teacher announced a new assignment and competition.

The boys loved competitions.
What could it be? -- they wondered.

"Class, we're going to memorize our times tables, all the way up to the tens," said the teacher.

The teacher explained that everyone in the class would take a test at the end of each week.

The kids would need to know all 100 math problems!

The top two students from each class would go on to the school's Championship Final in four weeks' time.

The four boys agreed to work together after school: they wanted to win!

TIMES TABLES
1x1=1
1x2=2
1x3=3
1x4=4
1x5=5
1x6=6
2x1=2
2x2=4
2x3=6
2x4=8
2x5=10
2x6=12
2x7=14
2x8=16
3x1=3
3x2=6
3x3=9
3x4=12
3x5=15
3x6=18
3x7=21
3x8=24
3x9=27
3x10=30
4x1=4
4x2=8
4x3=12
4x4=16
4x5=20
4x6=24
4x7=28
4x8=32
4x9=36
4x10=40
5x1=5
5x2=10
5x3=15
5x4=20
5x5=25
5x6=30
5x7=35
5x8=40
5x9=45
5x10=50
8x1=8
8x2=16
8x3=24
8x4=32
8x5=40
8x6=48
8x7=56
8x8=64
8x9=72
8x10=80
9x1=9
9x2=18
9x3=27
9x4=36
9x5=45
9x6=54
9x7=63
9x8=72
9x9=81
9x10=90
10x1=10
10x2=20
10x3=30
10x4=40
10x5=50
10x6=60
10x7=70
10x8=80
10x9=90
10x10=100

In just one day, Brilliant Bob discovered two things he wanted to learn and master: a wheelie, and the times tables.

At dinner Bob told his parents about his challenges.

"You're going to have to practice persistence like never before," said Bob's dad.

"Yes, practice and persistence make perfect," Bob's mom agreed.

Bob's parents felt sure Bob could learn the wheelie and represent his class in the final.

They'd witnessed his great focus and determination many times before.

Brilliant Bob and Dazzling Dave made their plan.

Every day after school, they would practice wheelies for one hour.

Then, they would go inside to do homework and have dinner.

After dinner the boys would meet at Bob's house for one hour of practicing times tables.

Brilliant Bob's mom had given Bob some very handy flash cards that would help them practice all 100 of the math equations.

They would need to practice, practice, and practice!

Persistence was a must.

Dave
Bob
HOMEWORK

5×8
9

The next day, Brilliant Bob and Dazzling Dave rushed from school to practice wheelies.

Just as they thought, it was harder than it looked.

They either pulled the front wheel up so high they had to drop their feet to the ground and run along with the bike, or they didn't pull up hard enough and barely got the front wheel off the ground.

It was very frustrating, and a little embarrassing.

"We must keep at it. We must keep at it," said Bob.

But, it was soon time to go in and do homework.

After homework, dinner, and a bit of help cleaning up, it was time for the four boys to practice the times tables.

They didn't have much time and they had 100 multiplication facts to memorize!

The boys found the flashcards really helpful.

They also used pencil and paper to write the times tables over and over again.

Every day they wrote the full set, starting with 1 x 1, all the way to 10 x 10.

They wrote until their hands were sore!

They also took mock tests and timed each other, and marked any equations they got wrong.

To win, they would have to be fast and accurate.

6x10
7x2
7x7
5x5
4x4
6x5
9x8
5x2
3x9
3x7
2x6
TICK
TICK

They did this same routine every day that week: wheelies and times tables.

The days and week flew by.

Brilliant Bob and Dazzling Dave had each managed to ride a wheelie for about 5 seconds.

They were pretty happy with that, but it would take much longer to ride the whole block.

And today was the first class test of the times tables.

The four boys were excited and nervous, but confident.

They knew they'd practiced with great *persistence* and focus.

It was 'show time.'

The pressure was on, but it was going to be fun.

The computers made it a cool way to compete.

All you had to do was type in the correct answer as fast as you could.

Ready, set, go!

Multiplication pairs of numbers flashed across each kid's computer screen and each kid typed their answers as fast as they dared.

1 x 3, 3 x 4, 5 x 6, 8 x 8, 2 x 6,

4 x 7, 7 x 5, 9 x 6, 10 x 10 and so on...

The test flew by, and the kids answered all 100 questions quickly. Everyone was focused and did their best.

8 x 4 = 32
3 x 7 = __
5 x 9 = __

The teacher checked the scores and times for each student on her master computer.

Brilliant Bob, Dazzling Dave, Genuine George and Superboy Sam were anxious.

Who would make it and who wouldn't?

The teacher read out the three best results.

"In 3rd place, it's...Superboy Sam."

"In 2nd place... it's Brilliant Bob."

"And in 1st place...it's Genuine George!"

3rd
2nd
1st

The boys were very happy.

Their hard work had paid off.

Brilliant Bob, Dazzling Dave, Genuine George and Superboy Sam repeated their winning formula.

Wheelie practice after school and times tables after dinner: every day!

Bob and Dave were up to 15-second wheelie rides.

And it felt awesome!

They could now imagine how it would feel to ride the whole block or more.

They would not give up.

They knew persistence was key to success.

TICK
TICK
7:15

The next Friday, the math class took another times table test.

As before, the teacher explained the rules and set up all the computers.

"Here we go!" she said, and she started the program that ran the test.

Again, the kids worked hard during the test and the time flew.

Who would win this time?

In 3rd place...it's Dazzling Dave.

In 2nd place... it's Genuine George.

And in 1st place... it's Brilliant Bob!

3rd
2nd
1st

The boys worked even harder on their challenges the next week.

They never missed a day of practice.

And no one was ever late.

Brilliant Bob and Dazzling Dave were getting more comfortable riding wheelies, but found they sometimes went too fast and had to put the front wheel back down.

They needed to learn to control the wheelie at slower speeds, so they could keep the wheel up and ride smoothly and steadily for longer.

It was soon Friday once again and time for the final class competition.

Who would be going to the Championship Finals?

The kids knew the drill. The test flew by.

It felt like time had stopped as they waited for the results.

Which two kids had scored the highest and best on all three tests?

This time, only the names of the two overall winners were called.

In 2nd place... it's Brilliant Bob!

In 1st place... it's Genuine George!

The class went crazy.

High five, Bob and George!

CHAMPIONSHIP FINALS
CANDIDATES
1st Place
George
2nd Place
Bob

Bob and George's total scores were very, very close.

All that practice and persistence had helped them win.

They knew the times tables. All 100 equations!

And although they both had done very well in the classroom tests, they knew they could still do better.

Most kids at this stage knew all the right answers, so speed in answering would make all the difference.

They would have to work even harder by practising more under time pressures if they wanted to win the Championship final.

And that's what Brilliant Bob set out to do.

He remembered what his mom had said that one night at dinner: "Persistence and practice make perfect!"

Bob was already practicing his wheelies after school every day, and reviewing his times tables after dinner every evening.

But, Bob knew he could do more. So, he asked his dad to practice with him too, before going to bed each night.

And that's what he did.

Talk about effort and persistence!

It wasn't easy and it wasn't always fun.

Bob was tired, but he wasn't going to give up.

The day before the Championship Final,
Bob and Dave practiced their
wheelies as usual after school.

Today felt like the day.

The boys rode side-by-side
to the starting point and both
pulled their front bike wheels
off the ground in unison as they began
to pedal in a very controlled manner.

On and on and on they rode on
one wheel; side by side.

The wheelies felt and looked perfect!

They rode the whole
block together with ease.

Sweet!

01

But they didn't have long to celebrate their joint triumph.

They still needed to practice for the math finals being held the next morning.

Brilliant Bob, Dazzling Dave, Genuine George and Superboy Sam all got together that evening to practice, but this time with speed.

Dave and Sam wanted to help Bob and George do their best!

And after his bath, Brilliant Bob and his dad practiced one more time too.

But that's not all.

Bob even got up early to quickly run through his flashcards one last time with his mother the next morning.

Brilliant Bob felt ready.

42!
42!
6x7
TICK
TICK
1:11

9x7=?
63!

24!
3x8

At school, Bob and the other finalists were sitting on the auditorium stage, each in front of a computer.

They would have to take the final test with all the other students watching.

It didn't take long because the finalists were the best, and they were very fast.

In less than four minutes, it was over.

The results were in. The school principal announced that one of the finalists had smashed the test.

Someone had gotten every single question right, in just under three minutes!

And... it was Brilliant Bob!

3x4
7x2
3x3
9x6
6x5
10x8
6x4
5x7
3x7
2x2

CLACK
CLACK

The crowd went wild.

Bob saw Dave and Sam in the crowd cheering, and George gave him a big thumbs-up from across the stage.

Genuine George was happy for Bob.

As Bob walked over to collect his trophy, he thought about all the hard work and persistence that helped him win this contest and master the wheelie.

Brilliant Bob knew that things have to be earned, and that they don't come easily.

It's really hard work committing to things you want to be good at.

There is no shortcut.

It's the only way.

Brilliant Bob had learned that persistence and practice really do make perfect!

Persistence is cool!

CHAMPIONSHIP FINAL

Brilliant Bob thanks you for reading this book.

He also invites you to join him in his other great adventures where:

Brilliant Bob is Competitive

Brilliant Bob is Strong

Brilliant Bob is Curious

Brilliant Bob Takes a Risk

Brilliant Bob is Stoic

Brilliant Bob is Brave

HIGH FIVE DUDE!

You can buy all seven books on Amazon.
And don't forget to visit Brilliant Bob's website at...

www.BrilliantBobKidBooks.com

Made in the USA
Monee, IL
21 November 2021

82680735R00029